Bridget Gadget

Selfie Sabotage

written by Mari Kesselring
illustrated by Mariano Epelbaum

www.12StoryLibrary.com

Copyright © 2015 by Peterson Publishing Company, North Mankato, MN 56003. All rights reserved. No part of this book may be reproduced or utilized in any form or by any means without written permission from the publisher.

12-Story Library is an imprint of Peterson Publishing Company and Press Room Editions.

Produced for 12-Story Library by Red Line Editorial

Illustrations by Mariano Epelbaum

ISBN
978-1-63235-037-4 (hardcover)
978-1-63235-097-8 (paperback)
978-1-62143-078-0 (hosted ebook)

Library of Congress Control Number: 2014937415

Printed in the United States of America
Mankato, MN
June, 2014

Table of Contents

Busy Bridget

"Man, you look beat," Eric said to Bridget. "You've got huge, dark circles under your eyes."

"Hey, knock it off," Bridget replied. "I don't want to hear how horrible I look."

Bridget and Eric were walking to school. They lived next door to each other and had been friends for as long as Bridget could remember.

"Stayed up late working on a paper for English," Bridget muttered. "*Romeo and Juliet.*"

She'd been up past midnight finishing it, then nearly slept through her alarm. Luckily she'd had enough time to print off the paper before rushing out the door.

Bridget took her phone out of her back pocket and took a quick selfie showing the exhausted look on her face. She posted it to SocCircle, her favorite social networking site. She added a note, *So tired. Up late writing bout R&J. Anyone else?*

Bridget wished Ms. Kaufman, her English teacher, would accept papers electronically like many of her other teachers. But Ms. Kaufman was old-fashioned. She didn't even allow e-readers. She thought a book needed to be made out of paper to be a real book.

Bridget showed her post to Eric.

"Yikes," he said. "You're set on your Halloween costume. You look like a zombie."

"Thanks," Bridget grumbled. So did her stomach. "You got a granola bar or something? I didn't have time for breakfast."

Eric swung his backpack to one shoulder and dug in the small front pocket. He pulled out a blueberry and granola snack bar and tossed it to Bridget.

"Thanks," Bridget said. She could always count on Eric to be prepared for the unexpected.

"I've just been busy with Palette," Bridget explained. Palette was Blue Lake Junior High's art club. "There's a lot of work to do for the showcase that's coming up. Tech Club and homework have been really crazy too."

"Sounds like you're barely keeping up," Eric said as they turned the last corner toward school. "Why are you in two clubs, anyway?"

"I want to get Blue Lake Honors this year," Bridget said. "My dad says he'll get me a new Lingo tablet computer this summer if I get the award. It comes with a totally cool laser-projected keyboard."

To get Blue Lake Honors, students had to participate in at least two school clubs, play at least one sport, earn a B average or higher, and display leadership and cooperation at school. It wasn't easy. But for a laser-projected keyboard, it was more than worth it, Bridget thought.

"Still," Eric said after a moment. "Seems like a lot of work to me."

"Did you not hear me say *laser-projected keyboard*, Eric? It's so awesome. You can project the keyboard onto a table or desk or even your lap!"

Bridget imagined how cool it would be to have such a futuristic gadget. Some of her teachers probably had never even heard of it, and she'd be the first at school to have a tablet like that.

Eric laughed. "I heard. But it still seems like a lot of work to me."

"I'm fine. I've got it all under control. Look," Bridget pulled up the calendar app on her smartphone. She showed Eric how she'd carefully scheduled all her activities and homework assignments.

"Any time for fun in there?" Eric asked.

Bridget rolled her eyes. "Who said I'm not having fun?"

An alert message popped up on Bridget's phone. Bridget's best friend, Emma, had posted a comment about Bridget's selfie on SocCircle.

Looks like a good pic for our art project, Gadget!

Emma had given Bridget the nickname Bridget Gadget a long time ago. Because of Bridget's love of all things tech, it was a fitting name. But she usually just called her Gadget for short.

Emma and Bridget were working on an art piece for Palette's showcase. It was a slideshow of selfies they'd taken. They'd used different filters to give each selfie a special effect and added text to them. There was a selfie of Bridget hugging her dog, Sunny, with a caption that read "puppy love," a selfie of Emma looking bummed after a bad grade on a science test with the word "grrrrrr!" in the space above Emma's head, and even a couple of snaps with Emma and Bridget together.

Bridget liked it when art meant something to someone looking at it. She hoped their piece in the showcase would make people think about what it was like to be a 12-year-old girl in the town of Cyber Hills. But Bridget and Emma still had a lot of work to do to finish the project.

"I'm just saying, you look tired," Eric repeated as they walked into the school building.

"The showcase is two weeks from now," Bridget said. "After that, things should slow down."

Tech Club Tycoon

When Bridget arrived at her locker, she found Emma waiting for her.

"Your selfie this morning was too funny! Were you really up late?"

"Super late. Did you finish your paper?"

"Yeah. I hope it's good." Emma sighed as she leaned against the row of blue lockers. "I know we've got Palette today. But can you meet tomorrow after school to work on our selfie project?"

"Tuesday?" Bridget flipped through the calendar on her smartphone. All she had for Tuesday night so far was science homework.

"You got it," Bridget said. She typed *Emma—selfie proj* into her calendar.

"Good, because we really need to get that done," Emma said. "I'm surprised Poua is even letting us include it in the showcase. I mean, we weren't exactly done by the submission deadline."

Poua Vang was president of Palette. The submission deadline for the showcase had passed a week ago. But Bridget had convinced Poua to let her and Emma include their work even though it wasn't quite done yet. Poua had agreed, only because she was really excited about their project.

"Poua's pretty strict about rules," Emma said.

"Really?" Bridget said sarcastically. Both girls, and many others around the school, thought Poua was bossy and hard to get along with.

"Yeah, we lucked out," Emma said as Bridget slammed her locker shut.

At lunchtime, Bridget was biting into her turkey sandwich, waiting for Emma to get through the long lunch line, when she felt a light tap on her shoulder. She turned to see Trevor, president of Tech Club.

"Oh hey," Bridget said, quickly swallowing her bite. "What's up?"

"I've got some official Tech Club business to talk to you about," Trevor said, sitting down next to her. "I know we meet on Thursdays, but I wanted to ask you about this before then."

"Uh, okay," Bridget said. Trevor was always school-oriented, so it didn't surprise her that he was using his lunch period to do something for Tech Club.

"The work I'm doing for the club is getting a little overwhelming," Trevor explained. "I need a vice president . . ." He paused, looking at Bridget.

"Wait, what? Me?"

"Are you interested?" Trevor asked. "The main thing I'd need help with is managing the blog. You'd be in charge of writing blog posts or picking members from the club to do them. Whatever works."

"Why me?" Bridget asked. She assumed Trevor had good reasons for picking her. But because Bridget's dad was Nick Grant, president of the big tech company Lingo, and pretty much everyone at the school knew it, she was sometimes afraid that she got picked for things because of him, instead of who she was. She wanted to be sure Trevor chose her for the right reasons.

"Bridget," Trevor said. "No one in this school knows tech as well as you do. Not even me. You always have a new gadget in your hands. Your experience and knowledge would really improve the quality of the blog."

Bridget thought about how busy she'd been with Palette, homework, and Tech Club already. But being a vice president would make her even more likely to get Blue Lake Honors, and one step closer to owning that new tablet. Plus, Bridget loved Tech Club. Managing the blog could be a lot of fun. And Trevor was right, she did know a lot about tech.

"Yeah, I'd love to," Bridget said. "I'm in."

"Great! The rest of the club will need to approve you as vice president, just so you know. We'll do a vote at Thursday's meeting. I'll text you with more details later."

As Trevor walked away, Emma set her lunch tray on the table and slid into the seat next to Bridget.

"What did Trevor want?" Emma asked, struggling to open her milk carton.

"Trevor's nominating me as vice president of Tech Club!" Bridget announced.

"Whoa! Awesome!" Emma gave her a high five. "Are you pumped?"

"Yeah, totally!" Bridget said, and she meant it. She just hoped she wasn't taking on too much. But she told herself it would all be worth it when she earned Blue Lake Honors and had her new tablet with the laser keyboard.

Madame President

After school that day, Bridget and Emma headed to the art room for the weekly Palette meeting.

"Poua's gonna be upset that we don't have our project done yet," Emma said as they sat down on the tall stools in the art room. The room always smelled like paint and pencil shavings.

"Well, we're gonna work on finishing it tomorrow night. We'll just tell her that," Bridget said. Sure, Poua was intense, but she wasn't completely unreasonable, Bridget hoped.

Just then, Poua sped into the art room, kicking up a trail of clay dust.

"Okay, you guys, time to get serious." Poua breezed to the front of the room where the art teacher stood during class. Her long, dark hair whipped around like a silk veil in a strong wind.

Emma nudged Bridget and raised her eyebrows, but Bridget kept her attention on Poua.

Most club presidents at Blue Lake didn't take their responsibilities too seriously. But Poua acted as though she'd been elected president of the United States.

Poua was also the best artist in the school. She'd won a lot of awards for her paintings, and many of her works decorated Blue Lake's classrooms. She had even painted a mural in the hallway by the gym. So, it made sense that she should be Palette's president.

Ms. Aller, the art teacher, was the teacher supervisor of Palette, but she adored Poua so much that she just let her run the show. Ms. Aller usually sat in the back of the room while Poua ran the meetings. She only chimed in if there were questions or problems Poua couldn't solve.

There was no doubt—Poua was a fantastic artist. But Poua's reputation for rules and being strict was probably the reason there were only six other members in Palette, including Bridget and Emma. Most of the club members had learned that it was useless to argue with Poua—she always had to have her way.

With the art showcase coming up, Poua had been even more demanding than usual. She wanted everything to be perfect.

"Now, listen up, the show's only a week and a half away. There's still a lot to do. And I have a plan for the Palette Wall."

The Palette Wall was a tradition for all Palette showcases. It was a special wall in the showcase that was dedicated to Palette members only. They got to use it for whatever they wanted. In the past, Palette members had made collages or self-portraits to represent everyone in the club.

Poua went on, "I'm doing a painting for the wall. It will be a montage of all the

club members' names in smooth script brushstrokes. I'll use mostly warm colors. It'll look great."

Bridget felt her phone vibrate and snuck a peek at it.

Isn't the wall supposed 2 b something the WHOLE club works on?, Emma's text read.

Bridget glanced at Emma and shrugged. Bridget looked around at the other members of art club. Evelyn Otto looked about to fall asleep, leaning her chin on her hand, her bangs falling in front of her face. Carlos Perez was doodling in his notebook. The other two members of Palette—Alyssa Lowe and Grant Jung—were using their smartphones. No one seemed that interested in having an opinion.

Poua went on, not seeming to notice or care that nobody was paying much attention to her.

"On to the next item of business." Poua plugged her laptop into the classroom digital whiteboard. She turned on the board, revealing a diagram of some kind.

"What's that?" Emma asked.

"This is a map of how we'll set up the showcase." Poua grabbed a digital whiteboard marker and started circling things on the map. "The sculptures will be here, in the southwest corner. Over here, we'll have paintings, then the drawings—"

"Excuse me," Bridget heard herself say.

"Yes?" Poua's face showed a mix of annoyance and surprise. People didn't interrupt her very often.

Bridget cleared her throat. Clearly Poua's excitement about the showcase was getting in the way of her letting anyone else have a say. The showcase was supposed to be group effort. *Someone* needed to speak up.

"I think it would be good if we could all plan together what the layout will be," Bridget said.

"Well, I already decided everything," Poua countered. She turned back to the whiteboard.

"I know," Bridget said. "But I think the whole group should be able to give their opinions. Same with the Palette Wall. We should talk about it as a group."

Poua set the marker down on the table in her front of her and leaned over it, glaring at the six club members. Her gaze fell last on Bridget.

"Does anyone have a problem with my plan?" Poua was smiling, but her eyes blazed behind her glasses.

Bridget looked around. It was clearly someone else's turn to stand up to Poua. Bridget couldn't be the only one who felt this way. In fact, she *knew* she wasn't. Bridget looked at Emma, waiting for her to say something. Anything.

But Emma looked down at the desk in front of her, just like the other four club members. Bridget glanced toward the back of the room, but Ms. Aller seemed to have stepped out of the classroom.

"So, Bridget," Poua said after a moment of eerie silence. "It sounds like you're the only one with a problem. If I were you, I'd spend less time questioning my ideas and more time finishing your project."

Bridget felt her face get red. Poua was being a control freak, but she was right about the project.

"Yeah, sure," Bridget said, and immediately regretted saying it. Poua was being totally unfair. And Bridget hated to think that Poua had won this one.

"You're lucky your project is good," Poua muttered. "And don't forget," Poua said more clearly to Emma and Bridget, "You guys had better have that slideshow done by the Friday before the showcase. Otherwise, it's *not* going in."

Then, as Poua went back to explaining the map and giving out orders, Bridget felt her phone vibrate in her back pocket again. She pulled it out and looked at the text. It was from Trevor.

Need blog post Tues nite.

Already? Bridget thought. Another text from Trevor appeared.

It'll help Tech Club decide if you'll be good as vice prez.

Bridget felt a headache coming on. She could feel the stress hitting her like a tidal wave, trying to knock her under. If the post was supposed to go live on Wednesday morning, she'd probably have to write it Tuesday night. But then, when would she finish the selfie project with Emma? Somehow, she'd have to make it work.

Art Monster

At home that night, Bridget started on her article for the Tech Club blog.
She decided to write a review of the painting app that she and Emma were using as part of their selfie project—PaintScript. PaintScript was a brand-new app from Lingo. It allowed users to place text on top of photos and add different effects to the text, so that the letters moved across the image or even glowed. The program could also create animations from a series of images.

Unfortunately, Bridget found that she had a lot to say about the app, so this was turning out to be a long blog post. Plus, she wanted it to be absolutely perfect. She knew she had a good chance of becoming vice president, but a good first blog post would seal the deal. She'd definitely have to work on it tomorrow after school. Emma would not be happy that she was bailing on their art project.

Just then, Bridget's phone buzzed with a text message. Bridget felt a chill run up her spine—it was a text from Poua. What did she want?

Not cool 2day. I'm the prez.

Bridget rolled her eyes. Since when did being president of Palette make you queen of the world? What was Poua's problem? Bridget didn't respond to Poua's text. Minutes later, another one came in.

Better get ur project done by next Mon. Might not be room in showcase.

Bridget's stomach did a flip. Poua had said they could have until next Friday to finish the project. Now, it had to be done by Monday? That didn't give them much time. Emma had been bugging Bridget to work on the project for weeks. She shouldn't have to suffer because Bridget was so busy.

What happened 2 nxt Fri? Bridget texted.

Poua texted back immediately, *We need it by Mon.*

Bridget wanted to throw her phone across the room. This was so unfair. Bridget knew she could talk to Ms. Aller, but she doubted their teacher would believe anything bad Bridget had to say about Poua. Bridget would have to handle this on her own—and she didn't have many options.

Bridget pulled up VidChat on her phone and called Emma. Emma's face appeared on the screen.

"You're up late again, Gadget," she said. Bridget was surprised to see that Emma was still wearing her school clothes.

"Yeah . . . about that . . ."

"What? Oh no, don't say it."

"I'm really sorry. I can't work on the project tomorrow," Bridget said, avoiding eye contact with Emma on the screen.

"We have less than two weeks to finish," Emma reminded her.

"It's actually worse than that . . ." Bridget said. She told Emma about her texts from Poua and watched as Emma's face shifted from annoyance to pure frustration.

"By Monday?" Emma yelled. "That wasn't the deal!"

"I know. I don't get what her problem is. But we'll get it done. We will." Bridget tried to sound confident, but she was a little worried. She'd promised Poua that they would have a least 50 different selfies in the slideshow. So far, they only had 30 ready.

"Do you want me to just finish it on my own?"

"No, I don't want to make you finish it alone. We're doing it together. "

Emma leaned her chin on her hand. "When?"

"Let me look at my calendar quick. Okay, here. How about Sunday? All day Sunday we work on it and get the whole thing done. Sound good?"

"Okay, but you'd better stick to it this time," Emma said. "If we don't finish, you're gonna be the one to face the wrath of Poua, right?"

"Totally. I'm not afraid of her," Bridget said. Then she wondered if that was true. If it was true that she really didn't care what Poua thought, she wouldn't have given up so easily when Poua switched the due date on her. And she would have stood up for herself and the rest of the group when Poua refused to hear their opinions about the showcase. She wouldn't have backed down the way she did.

Emma must have been thinking about the same thing because she said, "That was pretty gutsy of you to go head-to-head with the art monster today."

"I just thought it was dumb. The reason we're so crazy busy getting ready for the showcase is because we barely have any members. And you know why?"

"Duh. Art monster!" Emma laughed.

"You could've spoken up too," Bridget said after a minute.

"Gadget, not everyone wants to risk getting their head snapped off. And I need Palette for Blue Lake Honors too, you know."

"But she's being so unfair, and you hate it."

"I know, but it's not like she's gonna change."

Bridget sighed. Emma had a point.

Success!

"By now, you've all seen Bridget's fantastic post on the Tech Club blog," Trevor announced to the group at the meeting on Thursday. "I'd like to nominate Bridget Grant as vice president." Trevor motioned for Bridget to stand up.

Bridget felt a little silly standing up to be recognized as a potential vice president—everyone in Tech Club already knew her. But Trevor was big on ceremony.

"Do you have anything to say before we vote?" Trevor asked.

Bridget thought for a moment. She hadn't prepared a speech or anything. "Just that . . . well, you guys all know I love this club. I'd work hard to make our blog even better than it is now."

"We'll do an electronic vote on our site," Trevor explained as Bridget sat back down. Trevor turned on the classroom's digital whiteboard and pulled up the Tech Club website. "Everyone, log on to cast your vote now. We'll watch as the site tallies the votes."

The Tech Club members ducked their heads down over their smartphones and tablets as they voted. Bridget held her breath while watching two bars on the screen grow— red for no, green for yes. As the green bar grew longer and longer, Trevor again motioned for Bridget to stand.

"I'd like to introduce our new vice president—Bridget Grant!"

The members of Tech Club clapped and cheered. A few kids even jokingly snapped photos of Bridget with their smartphones.

She grabbed her smartphone and took a quick selfie in front of the digital whiteboard. She posted it to SocCircle with a note, *Voted Vice Prez of TC! So honored!* Bridget smiled. She was so glad to feel accepted in the club.

Trevor explained that Bridget would be managing the blog posts. He then moved on to other business. Tech Club was unlike Palette in almost every way. Tech Club had a bunch of members. And the members of Tech Club always seemed to be having a good time. They often hung out on weekends too. It wasn't just a school club, it was a group of friends—a community. Trevor was the president, but everyone had a voice.

As Bridget walked home after Tech Club, she got a text from Evelyn, a fellow member of Tech Club and Palette.

Can I write nxt blog post for Tech?

Bridget hesitated before texting back. She didn't know Evelyn that well, even though they were in a couple clubs together, and she wasn't sure Evelyn would do a good job writing for the blog. She knew Evelyn had never written a post before. What if she really messed it up? What if Evelyn wrote about digital cameras, chat rooms, or some other really old, boring technology? Not everyone in Tech Club knew tech as well as Bridget did. The only way to be sure the post would be perfect was to do it herself.

She texted Evelyn back, *Sry. Im gonna write nxt one.*

"There," Bridget said as she completed the last effect with PaintScript. "We're done!"

It was four o'clock on Sunday afternoon. Bridget and Emma had been working on their art project at Bridget's house since ten that morning.

"I can't believe we actually finished it," Emma said, looking stunned as she peered over Bridget's shoulder at the computer.

"Celebratory BFF selfie!" Bridget yelled as she flung her arm around her friend's neck and snapped a photo on her phone.

"Ha, look at your face!" Emma laughed.

"Whatever! Look at your face!"

"Hey, let's go see *Teen Warriors*. It's in 3-D at Cyber Theatre," Emma said. "We need to have some fun."

Bridget smiled. She hadn't been to a movie in ages, and she really wanted to see *Teen Warriors*. It was about a group of teenagers struggling to survive during an alien apocalypse. The teenagers ended up getting special powers from a friendly alien, and then they had to save the world from the invasion. The special effects in 3-D were amazing, and everyone at school was talking about it. Bridget checked her phone for show times.

"There's one at four thirty. We can make it if we bike," Bridget said. Cyber Theatre was just down the street from Bridget's house.

"Awesome! I thought for sure you were gonna bail on me and go finish some other really important thing," Emma teased.

Just then, Bridget got a text message. It was from Poua.

"Ah-ha!" Bridget shouted. "It's Poua. I can tell her we're done. She'll be shocked."

Need help making web banner ad 4 showcase. Ur techie. Come help.

Bridget showed the text to Emma.

"What do you think?" Bridget asked. "I really want to see that movie."

"Whatever," Emma said. "Just don't answer her. You deserve a break."

Emma did have a point, Bridget thought. She'd been thinking about nothing but Palette, Tech Club, and school for the past week.

Plus, Poua was asking for Bridget's help now because she didn't know how to create a web banner on her own. She only wanted Bridget's input because she couldn't do without it. After the way Poua had been treating everyone, Bridget thought it served her right.

Bridget texted back, *Sry. Have 2 help my dad 2nite.*

She turned back to Emma, "Let's go!"

As they raced out the door, Bridget glanced at a new text message from Poua.

R U sure U can't? Really need help. Please!

Bridget returned the text: *Sry. Can't.*

6

Called Out

"Why do 3-D glasses always make us look dorky?" Bridget said as she and Emma settled into their seats at the movie theater. The 3-D glasses were giant, covering half of Bridget's face.

"Whatever do you mean?" Emma asked. "Don't you think I look gorgeous in these?" Emma peered over the top of the frames of her 3-D glasses, puckered her lips, and fluffed up her short hair.

Bridget laughed. "Let's get a selfie of that for SocCircle." She pulled out her smartphone.

"Only if you do it too!" Emma said.

Bridget did her best to copy Emma's pose and snapped the photo of them together.

She posted the image to SocCircle, and added a note: *Looking good @ the movies w/ Emma Hein!*

The lights dimmed, and a cartoon bucket of popcorn danced across the screen, reminding everyone to silence and put away their phones.

"Wow," Bridget said as the lights in the theater came back on. "That was fantastic."

"The 3-D was so cool," Emma agreed as they made their way out of the theater.

"It's cool how they all had different powers," Bridget remarked. "I'd be the one with all the tech. Did you see all the hologram stuff? It's just like the laser keyboard on Lingo's new tablet!"

"Totally," Emma agreed.

Stepping outside into the sunlight, Bridget blinked from the brightness. As her eyes adjusted, she could make out the figure of someone with long hair walking their way.

Then, she saw who it was—Poua.

Bridget wanted to run, but it was clear that Poua had already seen her. In fact, Poua didn't look surprised at all to see her. She looked mad. Really mad.

"Great—here comes the art monster!" Emma whispered when she saw Poua.

"Oh, no," Bridget thought as she remembered the selfie she'd posted of herself and Emma at the movies. How could she have been so dumb? Poua must have seen the picture on SocCircle and then headed to the theater to bust her.

Poua stared straight at Bridget. "What happened to helping your dad?" she challenged, crossing her arms over her chest.

Bridget wanted to melt into a puddle on the pavement and trickle down the storm drain.

"Uh . . . I . . ." Bridget didn't know what to say. She'd been caught in her lie.

"I can't believe you lied to me, Bridget. I thought you really cared about Palette," Poua said.

"I do," Bridget said. "I just needed . . . a break."

"I guess Blue Lake Honors aren't very important to you either," Poua said. "It doesn't seem like you can handle the work."

"Hey, chill out," Emma said, taking a step toward Poua. "No one likes Palette, and it's all because of you. You just boss us around. It's all work and no fun. So don't blame Bridget."

"Too much work?" Poua's eyes were blazing. "Too much work for you? Are you serious? Do you know how much I do for Palette? And then, the one time I ask for help, I get lied to!"

"I'm sorry I lied," Bridget said, trying to defuse the situation. "I shouldn't have done that."

"Whatever," Poua said. "I know you guys don't like me. But tomorrow is the last meeting before the showcase this weekend. We still need to make the Palette Wall. How am I supposed to do that if I can't get anyone to help me? Maybe there won't be a showcase this year."

Bridget was stunned. No showcase? Would Poua really do that? Both Bridget and Emma could say good-bye to Blue Lake Honors if Palette wasn't able to pull off the only event the club held all year. That also meant no new tablet. No laser keyboard.

Before Bridget could respond, Poua whirled around and took off running.

Not So Different

"Oh my gosh," Emma exclaimed as Poua disappeared around the street corner. "What is her problem? She's nuts."

Bridget didn't say anything. She couldn't deny that Poua had a reason to be upset. Bridget had lied to her about her plans. And maybe Poua was right. Bridget had been really busy. Maybe Blue Lake Honors—and the laser keyboard—wasn't worth all this stress.

"I don't know," Bridget said finally as they got closer to her house. "I know she can be kind of a control freak. But I think she's trying to do what she thinks is best for Palette."

Emma scoffed. "What's best for Palette is for everyone to have *fun.* And we've never had that. I hardly know the other club members because Poua never gives us a chance to talk or anything. I mean, I think Carlos likes to draw. But I don't know if he likes to do anything else."

Bridget thought about Tech Club. Everyone knew each other. They were all friends, and they had a good time working together, even when there was a lot to get done.

Then Bridget thought about how she hadn't let Evelyn write a blog post because she was worried it might not be perfect. Maybe she and Poua had more in common than she thought. Maybe Poua's passion for art was like Bridget's obsession with technology. Thinking of it that way, it didn't seem fair to call Poua "nuts," because she was upset about something she cared deeply about.

Bridget pulled her phone from her back pocket. She had an idea that could bring Palette together.

Bridget texted Poua, *Ur right. You shouldn't have 2 do everything.*

Emma watched Bridget texting.

"You're texting her?" Emma was shocked. "After she was yelling at you? Why?"

"I want to help. And . . ." Bridget said. "I feel bad. I lied, so I should make it right. And you want there to be a showcase, right?"

"Of course," Emma said. "I just don't think she's gonna listen to you."

"I guess we'll find out," Bridget said.

"Good luck," Emma called as she turned the street corner to head back to her own house. "See you tomorrow."

As Bridget walked up her driveway, Poua texted back, *No one will help. They don't like me.*

Give me a chance, I can help w/ the wall, Bridget texted.

After a few minutes Poua finally texted back, *OK. How?*

Bridget smiled.

You'll see.

8

A Selfie Solution

On Monday after school, Bridget hurried to meet Poua a few minutes before the Palette meeting. Poua wanted to know what her plan was.

"Are you going to, like, lecture me about everything I've been doing wrong with Palette?" Poua asked when Bridget walked into the art room.

"No," Bridget said. "But you can't be rude to me, or I won't help at all."

Poua sighed. "Sure. What's your plan?"

"The Palette Wall is about bringing the members of Palette together. It's about everyone getting to know us," Bridget said. "So, we're going to get to know the real Palette—all the members."

"Okay, but how?" Poua leaned against the digital whiteboard, folding her arms across her chest.

Bridget pulled her laptop from her backpack and plugged it into the projector. "You'll see," she said. "But you have to trust me. Can you do that?"

Poua's eyebrows arched, and she shifted her weight from foot to foot. "Yes. I'll try. I just don't want anyone to think I can't handle being president . . ."

"I think part of being president is recognizing when you need some help," Bridget said.

Just then, Emma walked into the room, followed by the other members of Palette.

"Show time," Bridget said.

"Okay," Poua agreed, sitting on a stool next to Bridget. "I hope this works."

Bridget put her and Emma's selfie slideshow on the projector and clicked the play button. This got everyone's attention. Then Bridget started explaining her plan.

"Poua and I were just taking about how we don't really know each other that well. And, with a few days before the showcase, we still need a Palette Wall."

Bridget explained the selfie project and how she and Emma had used PaintScript to illustrate their selfies.

"Let's have a slideshow of selfies of all the Palette members projected onto the Palette Wall." Bridget had gotten this idea while thinking about the laser-projected keyboard she was so excited about. "That means everyone can have a say in how their own selfie looks. If Poua wants script letters, she's got them. Whatever you want. Everyone gets a chance to be creative. How does that sound?"

Everyone, even Emma, was staring blankly at her. Bridget frowned. She didn't expect applause, but she thought they could at least respond. Then, Bridget realized that they weren't looking at her; they were looking behind her—at Poua.

Everyone was too afraid to go against Poua.

"Poua," Bridget said finally. "What do you think of this plan?"

For a minute, it looked as if Poua wasn't going to say anything at all. But she seemed to realize that everyone was looking at her, waiting for something.

"I think . . ." Poua began slowly, "that Bridget's idea is great. But I guess I'd like to hear from all of you. What do you think?"

Evelyn was the first to speak up. "Could we add music to the slideshow? I think that would really make it cool."

"What about putting the Palette Wall at the front of the showcase instead of the end?" Grant suggested. "Then everyone could get to know Palette before even entering and seeing our work."

"I agree," said Emma. "If the wall is at the end of the showcase, they might miss it."

"We could add some personal info too," Alyssa added. "Like on our SocCircle profiles."

Before long, everyone was snapping selfies and using PaintScript to decorate them. The ideas were flying, and Palette was finally united.

9

A Perfect Palette

On the evening of the showcase that Saturday, all the Palette members were busy. They hung paintings, drawings, and other art on the bare white walls. They set sculptures and pottery up in the center of the room. Bridget and Emma's selfie project played on a loop in one corner. It was her favorite, not just because she and Emma had created it, but because it was the only display that used technology. Other than the Palette Wall.

Bridget was excited about the selfie slideshow everyone had created for the Palette Wall. Selfies of each Palette member, along with their name done in whatever style they wished, took turns lighting up the wall. As the slideshow looped, showing images of Bridget, Emma, Evelyn, Grant, and all the other club members, Bridget finally felt that Palette was really being represented.

Still, as people started to show up for the showcase, most of them seemed to want to talk to Poua about her paintings in the show. Poua didn't seem to mind the attention. But when Bridget took a break from wandering the showcase to get some water at the drinking fountain, she was surprised to see Poua leaning against a nearby vending machine.

"Are you hiding?" Bridget asked, mostly joking.

"Sort of," Poua admitted. Poua looked exhausted.

"You okay?" Bridget asked.

"Everyone thinks I have it so good," Poua said, shaking her head. "Like because I'm good at art, everything is easy. But it's a ton of work and pressure too. I'm really glad you and the other Palette members got involved in helping out." Poua hesitated, looking down at her feet. "I'm not great about letting other people help."

Bridget thought about the Tech Club blog, and she nodded. "I understand. I know what that's like," she said.

"Thanks, Bridget," Poua said. "I thought you were kind of whiny at first, but I guess you were just trying to help out."

"Ha!" Bridget had to laugh. "Whiny? I thought you were bossy."

Poua thought about it. "Well, I kind of was, I guess!"

"Feels like we need a selfie to capture this moment." Bridget leaned in close to Poua and snapped a photo. She posted it on SocCircle with the note, *Exhausted, but the Palette showcase was a success!*

"Okay, I'd better get back to the showcase," Poua said.

"I'll be over there in a minute," Bridget said with a smile.

Bridget knew it was time that she released some of her control over the Tech Club blog. Just like Palette, the Tech Club blog would benefit from multiple viewpoints and ideas. And Bridget simply didn't have the time to write every blog post herself and still have time for fun.

Bridget texted Evelyn, who was on ticket duty for the showcase. *Wanna write the nxt blog post?* she typed. *Could use ur help after all!*

Evelyn responded immediately, *Yea! Thanks! Want to write bout laser-projected keyboards. Think they r super cool.*

Bridget smiled. *AWESOME*, she texted.

Tomorrow, Bridget would work on figuring out some type of rotation so that everyone who wanted to got a chance to write a blog post. But for now, she wanted to go enjoy the showcase with the other Palette members. If she earned Blue Lake Honors, she'd be happy, and she'd have an awesome new tablet computer. But if she didn't have fun along the way, it just wouldn't be worth it.

The End

Think About It

1. Poua and Trevor are both presidents of clubs at school. How are the two characters alike, and how they are different? Which of the two do you feel makes a better president, and why?

2. Bridget posts a selfie of herself and Emma at the theater. Do you feel what she did was right or wrong? Be sure to explain your answer. Can you think of any other times when posting a photo online might be a bad idea?

3. In her art club meeting, Bridget acts confidently by standing up to Poua. Read another Bridget Gadget story and compare how Bridget acts in the two stories. Do you think she acts differently in the other story? Use examples to explain your answer.

Write About It

1. Do you participate in any clubs at school? Describe what you do in your favorite club and write about why you enjoy it. Do you have a special role in the club, such as president or vice president?

2. Imagine that you are a member of Tech Club and Bridget has asked you to write a blog post. Write about your favorite gadget. Describe what it does and why you think everyone should have one.

3. Write an alternative ending to this story, one in which Bridget decides not to help Poua at the end. What happens in your alternate ending? Does Bridget get her honors? Does the Palette Wall get finished on time?

About the Author

Mari Kesselring is a writer and editor of books for young people. She's written on various subjects, including William Shakespeare, Franklin D. Roosevelt, and the attack on Pearl Harbor. She is currently pursuing a Master of Fine Arts in Creative Writing at Hamline University. Like Bridget, Mari enjoys technology and new gadgets. She appreciates how technology provides unlimited access to knowledge and brings people closer together. Mari lives in St. Paul, Minnesota, with her husband and their dog, Lady.

About the Illustrator

Mariano Epelbaum has illustrated books for publishers in the United States, Puerto Rico, Spain, and Argentina. He has also worked as an animator for commercials, television shows, and movies, such as *Pantriste, Micaela,* and *Manuelita.* Mariano was also the art director and character designer for *Underdogs*, an animated movie about foosball. He currently lives in Buenos Aires, Argentina.

More Fun with Bridget Gadget

Cyber Poser
A former classmate, Olivia Bates, reconnects with Bridget on her favorite social networking site. But Bridget's not quite sure she remembers Olivia from way back in first grade. Using some online tricks and a new app that her dad's company designed, Bridget sets out to discover whether Olivia is a real friend or just a cyber poser.

Techie Cheater
For her birthday, Bridget gets a pair of high-tech glasses that can receive texts and take pictures. While wearing them, Bridget feels like a secret agent, and she is tempted to use them to cheat on a test, which opens up a whole new world of possibilities . . . and problems.

Tuned Out
Bridget's on a long road trip, squished between two of her annoying cousins. So she slips on her high-tech headphones and tunes them out. Problem is, she tunes everything out, including where she's supposed to meet up with everyone while visiting Mount Rushmore. With her phone battery dead, Bridget is left to find another techie way out of trouble.

READ MORE FROM 12-STORY LIBRARY

EVERY 12-STORY LIBRARY BOOK IS AVAILABLE IN MANY FORMATS, INCLUDING AMAZON KINDLE AND APPLE IBOOKS. FOR MORE INFORMATION, VISIT YOUR DEVICE'S STORE OR 12STORYLIBRARY.COM.